Almost Always Best, Best Friends

For my best, best friends.
You make every day better.

SIMON & SCHUSTER BOOKS FOR YOUNG READERS
An imprint of Simon & Schuster Children's Publishing Division
1230 Avenue of the Americas, New York, New York 10020
© 2022 by Apryl Stott • Book design by Chloë Foglia © 2022 by Simon & Schuster, Inc.
SIMON & SCHUSTER BOOKS FOR YOUNG READERS and related marks are trademarks of Simon & Schuster, Inc.
For information about special discounts for bulk purchases, please contact Simon & Schuster Special Sales
at 1-866-506-1949 or business@simonandschuster.com.
The Simon & Schuster Speakers Bureau can bring authors to your live event. For more information or to book an event,
contact the Simon & Schuster Speakers Bureau at 1-866-248-3049 or visit our website at www.simonspeakers.com.
The text for this book was set in ITC Usherwood Std.
The illustrations for this book were rendered in watercolor paint and digital ink.
Manufactured in China • 1121 SCP
First Edition
2 4 6 8 10 9 7 5 3 1
Library of Congress Cataloging-in-Publication Data
Names: Stott, Apryl, author, illustrator.
Title: Almost always best, best friends / Apryl Stott.
Description: First edition. | New York : Simon & Schuster Books for Young Readers, [2022] | Audience:
Ages 4–8. | Audience: Grades 2–3. | Summary: Best friends Poppy and Clementine learn to share their
feelings with one another after a new friend enters Clementine's life.
Identifiers: LCCN 2020050894 (print) | LCCN 2019028335 (ebook) |
ISBN 9781534499096 (hardcover) | ISBN 9781534499102 (ebook)
Subjects: CYAC: Best friends—Fiction. | Friendship—Fiction. | Emotions—Fiction.
Classification: LCC PZ7.1.S759 Alm 2022 (print) | LCC PZ7.1.S759 (ebook)
| DDC [E]—dc23
LC record available at https://lccn.loc.gov/2020050894
LC ebook record available at https://lccn.loc.gov/2020050895

Almost Always Best, Best Friends

APRYL STOTT

Simon & Schuster Books for Young Readers

NEW YORK   LONDON   TORONTO   SYDNEY   NEW DELHI

My name is Poppy and I am GREAT at being a best friend.

My best, best friend is Clementine.
When she comes over, we are never bored.

What if they're having fun doing all the things Clementine and I like to do?

What if Clementine thinks Georgia is a better best friend than me?

What if she never wants to play with me again?

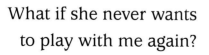

But then I dance away those thoughts. Clementine and I are best, best friends, after all. And there's no Poppy and Clementine's Bookmark Business without Poppy and Clementine!

What if?

WHAT IF?

What if?

WHAT IF?

WHAT IF?

Still, I have trouble falling asleep at bedtime.

I'm so relieved when Clementine invites me over to play the next day.

"Georgia is really good at braiding!" Clementine says.
"She can even do a French braid!"
I am not the best at braiding.
"I'm tired of doing hair. Let's pour tea for the ball," I say.

"Georgia is so good at pouring tea. She can lift the teapot this high!" Clementine says.

You know how when you're angry,
you're supposed to count to ten? I count
to one hundred as I wipe off my skirt.

"Let's work on our dance routine," I suggest.
"Georgia does her spins like this!"
Clementine says.
"I don't feel like dancing anymore," I say.

"Want to work on our bookmark business?" Clementine asks.
Finally, something Clementine can only do with me.

"Georgia draws all her lines perfectly straight," Clementine says.

"How do you know that?" I ask.

"Because we made some bookmarks yesterday. Do you want to see—"

"No!" I shout.

"I don't want to hear or see anything else about *Georgia*," I say. "I'm going home!"

At home, Dad gives me a big hug and lets me cry. When I can finally get the words out, I tell him what happened.

"The only way you're going to feel better is to talk to
Clementine about it," Dad says.
"But what if I say something that makes her not want to be my
best, best friend anymore?"

"A real best friend wants to know how you feel. Why don't we
practice what you're going to say, together?" Dad says.
"Okay," I agree.

"Clementine, I feel . . ."

"When you . . ."

"I would like for you to . . ."

"Poppy, it's not fair to ask Clementine to never play with Georgia."

"Terrible."

"Talk about everything Georgia does better."

"Never talk about Georgia again. And don't play with her either."

"But it would be easier if it was just the two of us again."

"Sometimes we're afraid of what's new," says Dad. "But new things can be good."

The next day, I go back to Clementine's house and all my words come out in a rush: "Clementine, I felt angry yesterday when you talked about all the things Georgia does better than me, and how you made bookmarks with her, because that's supposed to be our thing."

"There's something I want to talk to you about too," Clementine says. "Poppy, you hurt *my* feelings yesterday. I felt like you were ignoring me whenever I talked. And it made me sad when you yelled and left."

Seeing Clementine cry makes me want to cry too.
I didn't mean to hurt her feelings.

I take a deep breath and try again. "I'm sorry for the mean things I did and said when my feelings were hurt—I wish I could take them all back. I'll always be your best friend."

"I forgive you, and I'm sorry for hurting your feelings too," Clementine says.
"Georgia is waiting for me inside. Wanna come meet her?"

"Georgia, this is my friend Poppy," Clementine says proudly.

"Hello!" Georgia says. "I couldn't wait to meet you!
Clementine told me how great you are!"

"She told me all about you, too," I say.

"I made you a bookmark. Did Clementine give it to you?" Georgia asks.
"What bookmark?" I ask, surprised.
"That's what I was going to show you before you left yesterday. Here,"
Clementine says.
"Thank you, Georgia," I say. "I love it!"

Georgia is nothing like how I imagined her—she's even better!

There are still some things that I do better than Georgia and Clementine,

and there are other things that Georgia and Clementine do better than me.

But it turns out—

We are all GREAT at being best, best friends!